Captain Blownaparte and the Golden Skeleton
Part Four

by Helga Hopkins
Illustrated by David Benham

Published as an eBook in 2019
Paperback edition published in 2019

contact@blownaparte.com

ISBN-9781798924631

Captain Blownaparte™
and the Golden Skeleton

by Helga Hopkins & David Benham

Captain Blownaparte
and the Golden Skeleton
(Part Four)

Captain Blownaparte and his crew were tucking into a giant fish pie, but the golden skeleton was watching them very sadly. 'Don't be sad,' said Sproggie, 'once we find the rest of your golden bones you'll be human again and we'll celebrate with a lovely meal.' The skeleton sighed, 'The Ghost Captain has my leg bones, but nobody knows where his ship is.'

Clever Prosper knew what to do, 'We have to find Wilma the Whale, she knows all the gossip on the seven seas.' But when they found Wilma, she was in an extremely bad mood. 'I've got a terrible burning in my tummy, so buzz off and leave me alone!' she boomed. Then Swiss Sepp said that he knew what to do about it. 'My goat's milk will heal any burning tummy. So, if I sort out your tummy ache, will you lead us to the ghost ship?' That sounded good to Wilma, and she agreed straight away.

Swiss Sepp got a huge bucket of steaming milk from his goat Heidi. Sproggie and Pirate Rosie offered to carry the milk to the burning spot right inside Wilma. Prosper and Turnip offered to come along just in case they needed any help.

They moved deeper and deeper inside the whale, and it became darker and darker until they saw a red glow in front of them. As they came closer, they found an old sailor who had lit a fire. 'You can't light a fire inside a whale!' yelled Sproggie. 'Yes I can,' grumbled the old sailor, 'It's not my fault the silly old whale swallowed me.' Pirate Rosie didn't hang about and quickly emptied the bucket of goat's milk over the fire.

As they stood in the dark they heard a mighty rumble followed by an even mightier burp, and they were suddenly blown out of Wilma's tummy into the sea! Wilma was so happy, her burning tummy was healed, and true to her promise she led Captain Blownaparte to the Ghost Cliffs where the Ghost Captain could be found.

Nobody could understand why the golden skeleton was still unhappy. 'It's no good,' he grumbled, 'the Ghost Captain is never going to return my leg bones unless we give him something in return, and we don't have anything he wants.' 'I'm sure Prosper will know a way out,' said Captain Blownaparte, looking over at Prosper. The clever parrot nodded, 'The Ghost Captain has a very greedy ghost cat who he loves very much. If we lure the cat onto our ship with the smell of delicious food, we can tell the Ghost Captain that he can have his cat back in return for the golden leg bones.'

All the crew spent the rest of the day preparing the most wonderful dishes, and soon the scent of food was wafting through the air and spreading far and wide. But no ghost cat appeared. Meanwhile, Alfredo and Turnip were longingly watching all that lovely food. Eating was one of their favourite hobbies, and they grew more and more desperate to tuck into the lovely grub themselves!

'That bloomin' ghost cat isn't going to turn up, and all this lovely grub will be wasted,' grumbled Alfredo, as he grabbed a chicken drumstick. But as he was just about to bite into it, the drumstick suddenly disappeared and miraculously reappeared floating in mid-air inside a huge transparent ghost cat!

Everybody cheered, but while they'd been busy preparing for the ghost cat, they hadn't noticed that Captain Blownaparte's arch-enemy Captain Purplebeard had sneaked up on them with his cannons at the ready. Captain Purplebeard shouted across the water. 'Blownaparte! I'm going to sink you and your silly little ship once and for all!'

While everybody stood rooted to the spot in shock, Prosper whispered to the ghost cat. 'If you help me save our ship, we'll prepare a birthday feast for you every year.' The ghost cat looked at Prosper thoughtfully, and then with a huge smile on his face, he disappeared in a flash. A birthday feast each year was more than that greedy cat could resist!

The ghost cat reappeared on Purplebeard's ship and set to work. He tied Titch's sleeves behind his back, then snipped Muscles' braces so the big pirate was kept busy keeping his trousers up! Gertie was next, he pulled her scarf over her eyes so she couldn't work the cannons. Then the ghost cat chased the rest of the pirates high up on the ship's mast.

Captain Purplebeard was screaming angrily, but not for long, Prosper had gathered all his seagull friends together and they flew low over Purplebeard and completely covered him in bird poop! It wasn't a pretty sight. 'I can't stand all this,' screamed Captain Purplebeard, 'let's rush back to the harbour.' With that, the nasty pirates sailed away as fast as they could.

A jubilant crew greeted Prosper and the ghost cat back on their ship. The ghost cat didn't pause a second before he started tucking in again. 'I hope the ghost captain is going to bring me my legs,' sighed the golden skeleton, 'I'd love to be a normal seaman again.'

Sproggie suddenly squeaked and pointed at the horizon, where a large ghostly sailing ship was making its way towards them. The ghost cat looked up and meowed but didn't bother to stop eating. Soon the ghost ship sailed nearer and everybody became very nervous. Captain Blownaparte shouted across the water. 'You can have your cat back in return for the golden leg bones and we'll invite you to our big feast as well.'

In moments the ghost captain appeared on deck clutching a pair of golden leg bones. He gave them to the golden skeleton who at last became whole again and turned back into a handsome young man. There were tears and hugs all around and then the feast started in earnest.

Everybody was eating, singing and dancing. Then, when the ghost cat could finally eat no more, he and Prosper danced on the deck together. Captain Blownaparte giggled until he had tears in his eye, 'Now I've seen it all,' he spluttered, 'a cat dancing with a bird!

PEDRO   ROSIE   CAPTAIN   SPROGGIE
                              BLOWNAPARTE

PROSPER   SPIKE

PIRATE TIDY   ALFREDO   SWISS SEPP

TURNIP

Manufactured by Amazon.ca
Bolton, ON